For Joan Read

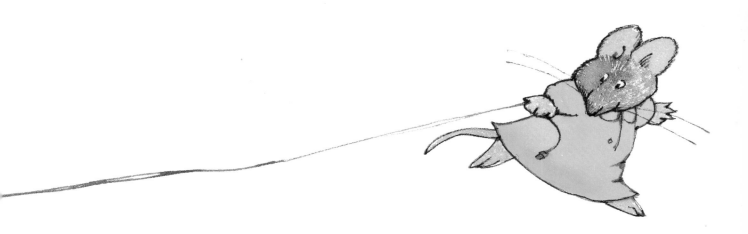

Jack had dinner early,

Noisy Nora

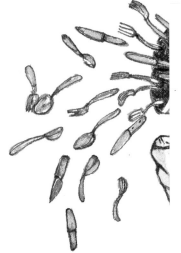

P1-3

WITH ALL NEW ILLUSTRATIONS
ROSEMARY WELLS

Picture Corgi Books

A PICTURE CORGI BOOK : 0 552 545902

First published in the United States in 1997 by Dial Books for Young Readers
Published in Great Britain by Doubleday, a division of Transworld Publishers Ltd

PRINTING HISTORY
Doubleday edition published 1998
Picture Corgi edition published 1999

1 3 5 7 9 10 8 6 4 2

Picture Corgi Books are published by Transworld Publishers Ltd,
61-63 Uxbridge Road, Ealing, London W5 5SA,
in Australia by Transworld Publishers, c/o Random House Australia Pty Ltd,
20 Alfred Street, Milsons Point, NSW 2061,
in New Zealand by Transworld Publishers, c/o Random House New Zealand,
18 Poland Road, Glenfield, Auckland,
and in South Africa by Transworld Publishers, c/o Random House (Pty) Ltd,
Endulini, 5a Jubilee Road, Parktown 2193

Printed in Belgium

Father played with Kate,

Jack needed burping,
So Nora had to wait.

First she banged the window,

Then she slammed the door,

Then she dropped her sister's marbles
on the kitchen floor.

"Quiet!" said her father.
"Hush!" said her mum.

"Nora!" said her sister,
"Why are you so dumb?"

Jack had gotten filthy,

Mother cooked with Kate,

Jack needed drying off,
So Nora had to wait.

First she knocked the lamp down,
Then she felled some chairs,

Then she took her brother's kite

And flew it down the stairs.

"Quiet!" said her father.
"Hush!" said her mum.

"Nora!" said her sister.
"Why are you so dumb?"

Jack was getting sleepy,

Father read with Kate,

Jack needed singing to,
So Nora had to wait.

"I'm leaving!" shouted Nora,
"And I'm never coming back!"

And they didn't hear a sound
But a tralala from Jack.

Father stopped his reading.
Mother stopped her song.

"Mercy!" said her sister,
"Something's very wrong."

No Nora in the cellar.
No Nora in the tub.

No Nora in the mail box
Or hiding in a shrub.

"She's left us!" moaned her mother
As they sifted through the trash.

"But I'm back again!" said Nora

With a monumental crash.